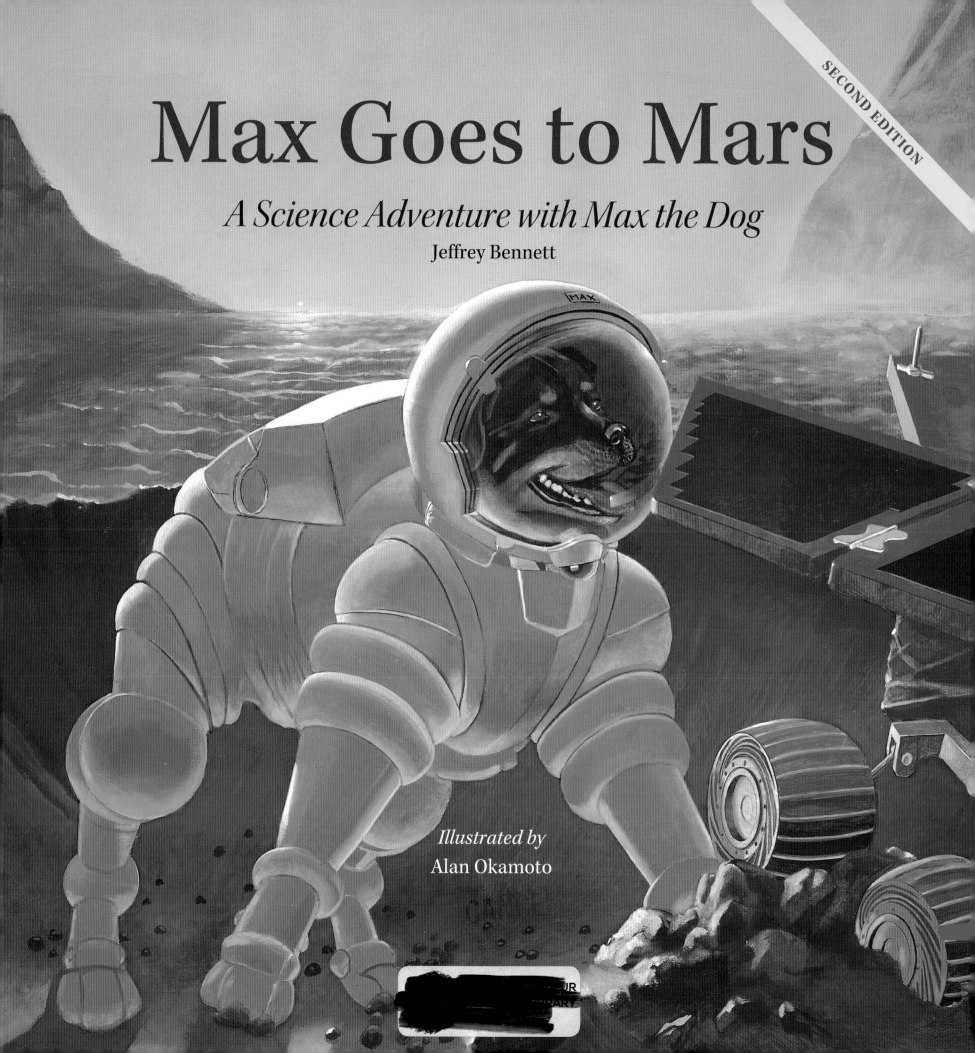

Max Goes to Mars

A Science Adventure with Max the Dog

Jeffrey Bennett

Illustrated by
Alan Okamoto

To Children Around the World:

Believe in yourself, believe in your dreams, and work hard to create a world in which we can all live together in peace as we reach for the stars.

About the New Edition

This second edition of *Max Goes to Mars* contains a set of fully updated Big Kid Boxes designed to incorporate the latest scientific discoveries about Mars.

Editing: Joan Marsh, Mary Douglas
Design and Production: Mark Stuart Ong, Side By Side Studios

Published in the United States by
Big Kid Science
Boulder, Colorado
www.BigKidScience.com

ISBN: 978-1-937548-44-5

Expert Reviewers

Dr. Nathalie Cabrol, NASA Ames Research Center
Eddie Goldstein, Denver Museum of Nature & Science
Dr. Steve Lee, Denver Museum of Nature & Science
Mark Levy, Educational Consultant
Dr. Christopher McKay, NASA Ames Research Center
Dr. Cherilynn Morrow, Aspen Global Change Institute
Dr. Nicholas Schneider, University of Colorado, Boulder
Joslyn Schoemer, Denver Museum of Nature & Science
Dr. John Spencer, Southwest Research Institute
Dr. Alan Stern, Southwest Research Institute
Dr. Henry Throop, Southwest Research Institute
Dr. Mary Urquhart, University of Texas, Dallas
Helen Zentner, Educational Consultant

Special Thanks To:

Maddy Hemmeter for modeling as Tori.

Lado Jurkin for modeling as Commander Grant. Mr. Jurkin is one of thousands of "Lost Boys of Sudan," children orphaned by war who then spent years trekking through African wilderness and living in refugee camps before finding new homes in the United States. The true story of the Lost Boys is an inspiration to all of us.

The children and teachers of P.S. 117 (Queens, New York City) for reviewing the book in draft form.

Story Time From Space for selecting this book to be read aloud from the International Space Station; video at www.storytimefromspace.com.

Also by Jeffrey Bennett

For children:
> Max Goes to the Space Station
> Max Goes to the Moon
> Max Goes to Jupiter
> The Wizard Who Saved the World

For grownups:
> Beyond UFOs
> Math for Life
> What Is Relativity?
> On Teaching Science

Textbooks:
> The Cosmic Perspective series
> Life in the Universe
> Using and Understanding Mathematics
> Statistical Reasoning for Everyday Life

This is the story of how Max the Dog helped humanity take the next giant leap — far beyond the Moon, to the wondrous planet Mars.

3

It had been only a few years since Max and his friend Tori helped start the Moon colony. Thousands of people had already visited the Moon, but no one had yet traveled beyond.

Tori and Max stayed busy at home on Earth. Tori was in school, and Max would play all day.

4

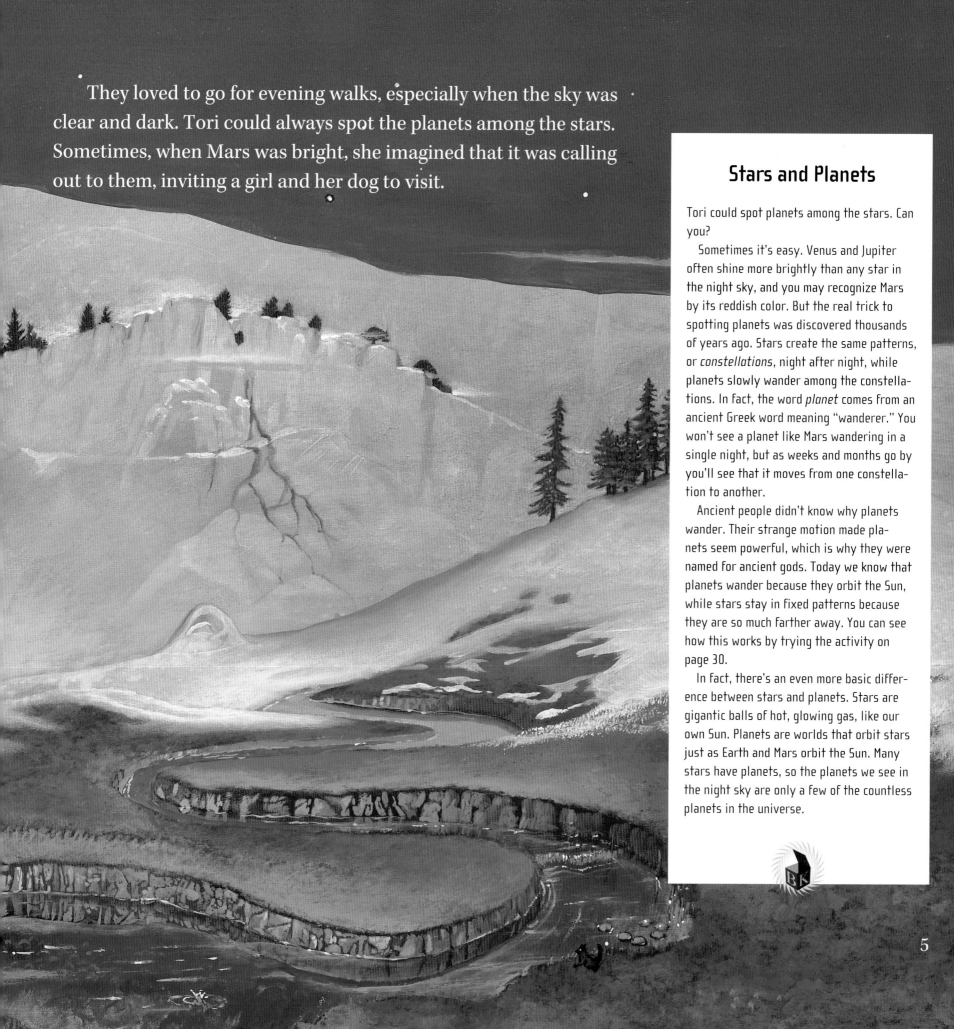

They loved to go for evening walks, especially when the sky was clear and dark. Tori could always spot the planets among the stars. Sometimes, when Mars was bright, she imagined that it was calling out to them, inviting a girl and her dog to visit.

Stars and Planets

Tori could spot planets among the stars. Can you?

Sometimes it's easy. Venus and Jupiter often shine more brightly than any star in the night sky, and you may recognize Mars by its reddish color. But the real trick to spotting planets was discovered thousands of years ago. Stars create the same patterns, or *constellations*, night after night, while planets slowly wander among the constellations. In fact, the word *planet* comes from an ancient Greek word meaning "wanderer." You won't see a planet like Mars wandering in a single night, but as weeks and months go by you'll see that it moves from one constellation to another.

Ancient people didn't know why planets wander. Their strange motion made planets seem powerful, which is why they were named for ancient gods. Today we know that planets wander because they orbit the Sun, while stars stay in fixed patterns because they are so much farther away. You can see how this works by trying the activity on page 30.

In fact, there's an even more basic difference between stars and planets. Stars are gigantic balls of hot, glowing gas, like our own Sun. Planets are worlds that orbit stars just as Earth and Mars orbit the Sun. Many stars have planets, so the planets we see in the night sky are only a few of the countless planets in the universe.

Dogs in Space

The real dog Max has never been to space, but other dogs have. A Russian dog named Laika was the first. In fact, she was the first living creature sent into space.

Laika was launched into Earth orbit aboard a ship called Sputnik 2 on November 3, 1957. Her trip provided valuable data that later helped people and other animals survive in space. Sadly, her own ship was not designed for a return trip home, and she died in space.

Twelve other Russian dogs made space launches and eight of them returned safely. The first dogs to survive a space flight were Belka and Strelka, who orbited Earth for a day on August 19, 1960. Strelka later had puppies. In an early example of space exploration helping to foster peace, Soviet leader Nikita Krushchev gave one of Strelka's puppies to the family of U.S. President John F. Kennedy. The last dogs in space — at least so far — were Verterok and Ugolyok. In 1966, they spent 22 days in space before returning home.

The United States never sent dogs into space but did send monkeys and chimpanzees. The first chimp, named Ham, made a short flight into space on January 31, 1961. He survived the flight and lived in zoos for the rest of his life.

* * *

Watch the real Max's merry-go-round trick at www.BigKidScience.com/maxvideo.

Tori got the phone call when Max was out doing his famous merry-go-round trick. As a puppy, he'd learned to spin the merry-go-round on his own, jumping on and off and sometimes just riding around. He still loved the trick, and kids usually came to ride with him.

"It's Commander Grant," said Tori. "They want a dog to go along on the first trip to Mars." Max just kept on playing.

Tori was both happy and sad. Happy that Max would get to go on such a great adventure. Sad because she knew that this time he'd have to go without her.

Tori remembered visiting a scale model of the solar system in Washington, DC. She learned that even when it's closest to Earth, Mars is about 150 times as far away as the Moon. The trip to Mars would take too long for a girl still in school.

How Far Is Mars?

The vast distances between the planets are easier to think about if we use a scale model of the solar system. The painting on this page shows part of a model, called *Voyage*, located outside the National Air and Space Museum in Washington, DC. *Voyage* shows the solar system at *one ten–billionth* of its actual size. The Sun is the gold ball on the pedestal at the right. The other pedestals show the locations of the four inner planets.

The models of the planets are inside the glass disks on each pedestal. Earth is about the size of a pinhead and shares its glass disk with the even smaller Moon. The Earth–Moon distance is only about 4 centimeters (1½ inches) in the *Voyage* model. Now, notice that the pedestal for Mars is several big steps beyond Earth. That's how Tori learned that Mars is so much farther away than the Moon.

If you want some real numbers, here they are: The Moon is about 380,000 kilometers (235,000 miles) from Earth. The distance from Earth to Mars ranges between about 56 and 400 million kilometers (35 and 250 million miles), depending on where the two planets are located in their orbits.

Learn more about *Voyage* and the scale of space at www.BigKidScience.com/Voyage.

Tori thought Max should know a little about his destination. "Listen carefully, Max. We call Mars the Red Planet because it looks like a reddish dot in the night sky. Long ago, people of many cultures gave Mars different names and made up stories about it. The name Mars comes from the ancient Roman god of war."

Max sat very still, staring right past Tori. "Good, I can see that you're listening," she said.

The Names of Mars

Mars was named for the mythological god of war more than 3,000 years ago, perhaps because its color reminded people of blood. Different people of the ancient Middle East had different names for the god of war, and each gave this name to the planet. The Babylonians called it Nergal, the Greeks called it Ares, and the Romans gave it the name Mars.

People in other parts of the world had different ideas about Mars. In India, Mars was known as Mangala and associated with a six-headed, warlike god. It was the "great star" to the Pawnee people of North America. The Chinese called Mars the "fire planet" or *Ying huo*, which translates roughly as "sparkling deluder." Even today Mars has many names in different languages.

Did you know that Mars has a day, a month, and a city named for it? Tuesday is "Mars day," as you can tell if you know how to say Tuesday in Spanish (Martes), French (Mardi), or Italian (Marte). We get the English Tuesday from the ancient Norse god of war, who was named Tiw. The month named for Mars is probably obvious: March. The city is Cairo, capital of Egypt, whose name comes from an ancient Arabic name for Mars.

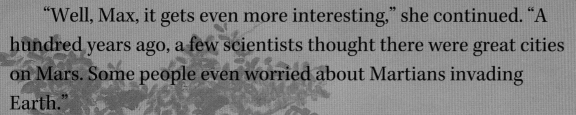

"Well, Max, it gets even more interesting," she continued. "A hundred years ago, a few scientists thought there were great cities on Mars. Some people even worried about Martians invading Earth."

"Can you imagine that?" Tori laughed. Max was definitely imagining something.

Martian Fantasies

Have you ever wondered why people often talk about Martians but rarely talk about, say, Venusians or Jupiterians? It started with blurry images of Mars seen through telescopes more than 100 years ago.

In 1877, an Italian astronomer named Giovanni Schiaparelli thought he saw straight lines on Mars. He called them *canali*, meaning "channels." However, the word was translated into English as *canals*, which made people think of artificial waterways. In 1894, an American astronomer named Percival Lowell opened his own observatory to study the canals of Mars. The Lowell Observatory is still used for astronomical research. You can visit it in Flagstaff, Arizona.

Lowell made detailed maps of Martian canals, imagining that they were built by an old civilization to transport precious water on a dying planet. H.G. Wells used this idea when he wrote about Martians invading Earth in his novel *The War of the Worlds.*

Of course, we now know that Lowell's idea had a major problem: The canals don't really exist. So what was he seeing? Remember that Lowell was looking by eye at blurry telescopic images of Mars. Perhaps he allowed his mind to fill in straight lines along blurry boundaries of light and dark geographical regions.

Missions to Mars

How can we know so much about Mars when no one has ever been there? The answer is that we've sent "robotic" spacecraft that use onboard computers to control their engines, cameras, and scientific instruments. We use radio waves to send them computer instructions and to receive back the pictures and data they collect. It works just like sending pictures or data with a cell phone, except over a much greater distance.

The first spacecraft to visit Mars was Mariner 4, which made a single flyby in 1965. Six years later, Mariner 9 became the first spacecraft to orbit Mars. The first successful Mars landings came in 1976 with the spacecraft Viking 1 and Viking 2.

Today, more than 20 nations are involved in robotic missions to Mars. Missions to study Mars from orbit include India's Mars Orbiter Mission (MOM) and NASA's MAVEN mission, both of which reached Mars in 2014. Ground missions include the robotic rovers Spirit (pictured on the cover and on page 18) and Opportunity, both of which landed on Mars in 2004, and Curiosity, which landed in 2012.

The paintings of Mars in this book are based on real data from Mars missions. The painting on this page is based on a diorama at the Denver Museum of Nature & Science, and the big TV on the right-hand page shows a view from the Spirit rover.

Tori took Max to a science museum, where they walked through an exhibit of Mars. "We know a lot about Mars now," she explained, "because many nations have sent spacecraft to Mars. But none of these spacecraft have carried any people or animals. That's why your trip is going to be so exciting."

Tori suddenly became more serious. "Max, there aren't any cities or Martians on Mars, but you could still help us make one of the greatest discoveries in history."

"Mars is a cold, dry planet today," continued Tori, "but scientists think that Mars had lakes and rivers a long, long time ago. There might still be water underground. And if there's water, well, maybe there's life!"

"Martian life would probably be too small to see without a microscope. Still, if you found even the tiniest living creature on Mars, we'd finally know for sure that we are not alone in the universe."

Max sniffed excitedly at the floor, proving that he was well-equipped for the search for microscopic life.

Water on Mars

Tori says Mars is dry today but had water in the past. How does she know?

Mars has to be dry today because its air is too thin for liquid water to last on its surface. If you took a cup of water outside on Mars, all the water would quickly either freeze or evaporate. But photographs from Martian orbit show dried up riverbeds, vast flood plains, and perhaps even dry lake beds and oceans. Studies of rocks by Mars rovers confirm that Mars once had lots of liquid water.

The era of abundant water is long gone. By studying craters on Mars, scientists can tell that most of the lakes and rivers dried up at least 2 billion years ago. However, Mars still has lots of frozen water ice in its polar caps and underground. Some of this ice may occasionally melt and flow for a short time. For example, flowing water may explain gullies on crater walls, like those shown in the painting on page 19.

More important to the search for life, the abundant ice means that some liquid water may still exist underground. This may be especially true near ancient volcanoes (see page 22), which might still generate enough heat to melt ice.

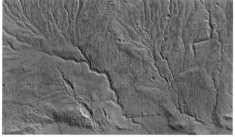

This photo, taken from Martian orbit, shows dried up riverbeds on Mars.

To Mars and Back

Are you wondering why the Mars trip takes so long? It's because of the way Earth and Mars orbit the Sun. Earth takes one year to orbit the Sun. Mars takes longer because it orbits more slowly and at a greater distance from the Sun. Like two people racing in different lanes around a track at different speeds, Earth passes Mars about every two years (more precisely, about every 26 months).

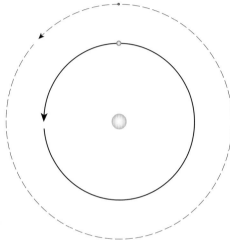

Earth and Mars line up in their orbits about every two years.

It's much easier to send a spacecraft to Mars if we time the trip to these orbital alignments. Otherwise, the trip would require far more fuel and expense. Even so, current spacecraft take 6 or more months to reach Mars. The 4-month trip in this story assumes the use of a more advanced spacecraft. By the time the crew reaches Mars, Earth will have raced ahead in its orbit. Unless the crew returned almost immediately, they'd need to stay until the next line-up about two years later.

As launch day approached, Tori and Max left Earth and returned to the Moon colony, where the Mars ship was waiting.

Tori could not hide her tears as she gave Max a big good-bye hug. She knew that Mars lines up with Earth in its orbit only about every two years. Max and the crew would have to stay on Mars almost that long before they could return home.

Commander Grant saw the concern on Tori's face. "Don't you worry," he said, "we tested everything over and over again. It will be a long trip, but we'll all be fine."

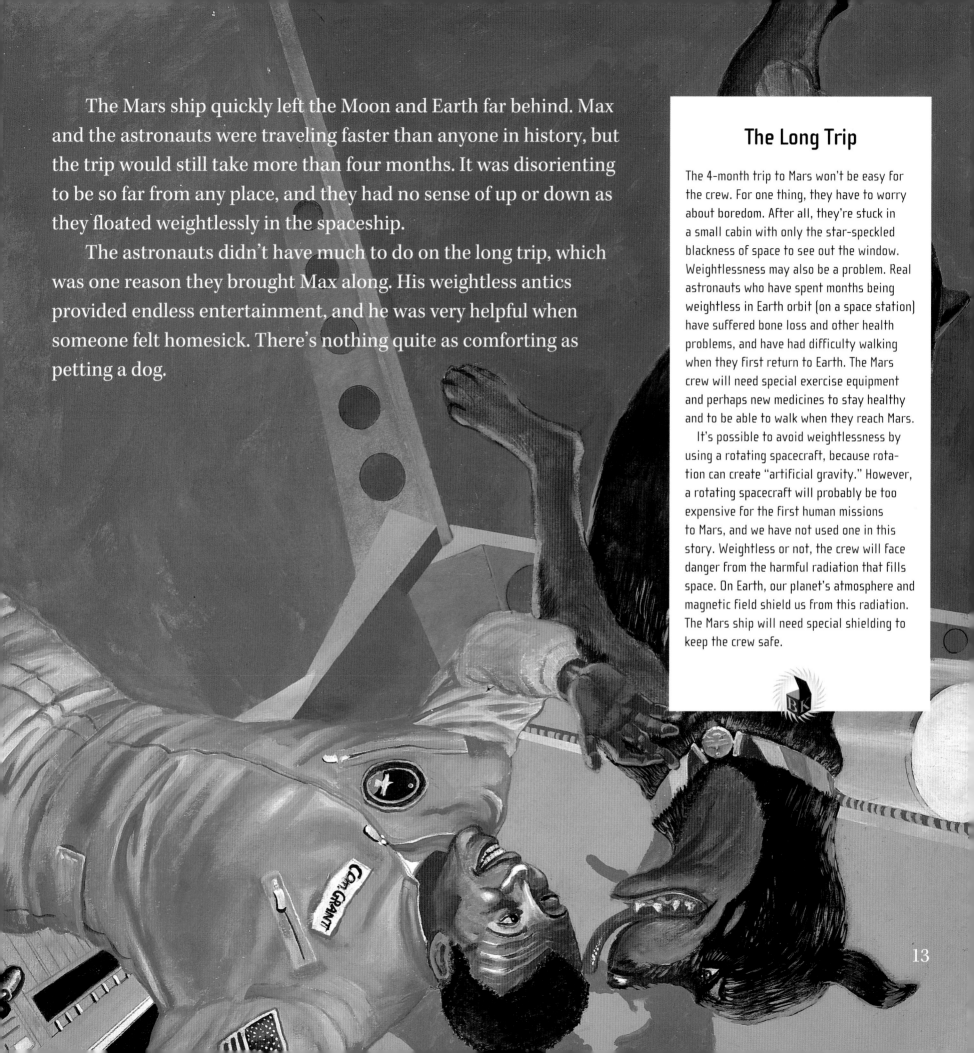

The Mars ship quickly left the Moon and Earth far behind. Max and the astronauts were traveling faster than anyone in history, but the trip would still take more than four months. It was disorienting to be so far from any place, and they had no sense of up or down as they floated weightlessly in the spaceship.

The astronauts didn't have much to do on the long trip, which was one reason they brought Max along. His weightless antics provided endless entertainment, and he was very helpful when someone felt homesick. There's nothing quite as comforting as petting a dog.

The Long Trip

The 4-month trip to Mars won't be easy for the crew. For one thing, they have to worry about boredom. After all, they're stuck in a small cabin with only the star-speckled blackness of space to see out the window. Weightlessness may also be a problem. Real astronauts who have spent months being weightless in Earth orbit (on a space station) have suffered bone loss and other health problems, and have had difficulty walking when they first return to Earth. The Mars crew will need special exercise equipment and perhaps new medicines to stay healthy and to be able to walk when they reach Mars.

It's possible to avoid weightlessness by using a rotating spacecraft, because rotation can create "artificial gravity." However, a rotating spacecraft will probably be too expensive for the first human missions to Mars, and we have not used one in this story. Weightless or not, the crew will face danger from the harmful radiation that fills space. On Earth, our planet's atmosphere and magnetic field shield us from this radiation. The Mars ship will need special shielding to keep the crew safe.

13

Back on Earth, Tori had a special privilege: Each day before school, she received a private video phone call from the crew.

During a call one day, about halfway through the voyage to Mars, Commander Grant pointed his camera out the window to show Tori the tiny Earth and Moon in the distance. "That's where you are," he said.

"Not just me," she thought. "Every person who has ever lived grew up on that tiny blue dot."

Light-Travel Time

Tori's phone calls keep her in touch with the crew, but conversations aren't easy. The problem is the time that it takes for light to travel between Earth and the Mars ship.

The radio waves we use to communicate with spaceships are actually a form of light, even though we can't see them. Like all other forms of light, radio waves travel through space at the speed of light, which is 300,000 kilometers per second (186,000 mi/s).

That's really fast. If radio waves went in circles, they could circle Earth almost eight times in just one second! But distances in space are so vast that even light takes a long time to cross them. For example, radio waves would take about 6 minutes in each direction when the Mars ship is halfway to Mars. So if Tori asks "How are you?," she'll have to wait about 12 minutes for an answer: 6 minutes for her message to reach the crew and 6 more minutes for their response to get to Earth.

The astronauts were very happy when Mars finally began to loom large ahead of them. They had all spent time on the Moon, but this was different. Mars is much bigger than the Moon, though still much smaller than Earth. It even has two moons of its own, named Phobos and Deimos, but they are so small that they look more like rocks than worlds.

Mars and Its Moons

Do you want to know exactly how big Mars is? Its diameter is about 6,800 kilometers (4,200 miles), or about half that of Earth. The picture below shows the two planets to scale. Interestingly, because most of Earth's surface is covered by oceans, Earth's land area is about the same as the land area of Mars. That means exploring all of Mars would be like exploring all of Earth's continents combined.

The two moons of Mars, which are named for two children of the mythical god of war, are very different from our own Moon. Our Moon is round and almost as big as some planets. Mars's moons are shaped more like potatoes and they are very small. Phobos is only about 13 kilometers (8 miles) across. Deimos is even smaller — about 8 kilometers (5 miles) across. These tiny moons have such weak gravity that if you stood on them, a big jump would almost allow you to escape into space. They also orbit Mars quite closely and quite fast. Phobos takes only about 8 hours to orbit Mars, and Deimos takes just over a day. You can see both moons in the painting on this page: Phobos is clearly visible and Deimos is the bright dot near the lower right.

The descent to Mars was scary but fun. For a few long minutes the ship blazed through the thin Martian atmosphere. Then the crew opened the ship's parachutes to slow down. Finally, they used small rockets to zero in on the landing site. The equipment for their base camp was already there, because it had been sent to Mars two years earlier.

After four months in a small spaceship, Max and the astronauts were eager to get outside. It looked almost Earth-like, but they knew they'd have to wear spacesuits to survive.

Don't Forget Your Spacesuit!

Do you know why you'd need a spacesuit on Mars? There are at least four good reasons:

First, the air on Mars is so thin that it would feel much more like the airless Moon than even the highest mountaintops on Earth. People need much greater air pressure to survive. Second, the air on Mars has no breathable oxygen — it's almost entirely carbon dioxide. Third, the lack of oxygen means there's no ozone layer on Mars. On Earth, the ozone layer protects life from ultraviolet radiation from the Sun. Because Mars has no ozone layer, you'd need protection against this dangerous radiation. Fourth, Mars is very cold, with an average temperature of about −50°C (−58°F), and the thin air holds so little heat that it would feel even colder against your skin.

For all these reasons, you couldn't live more than a minute or so if you went out without a spacesuit on Mars. You'd only be safe in a pressurized environment like that in a spaceship, base camp, rover, or spacesuit.

The crew spent a few weeks recovering from the effects of weightlessness and preparing their base camp. They tended to the plants in the greenhouses. They checked the air and water recycling systems. Most important, they set up a factory to make the rocket fuel they would need to leave Mars.

As usual, Max entertained everyone. He loved playing in the weak gravity of Mars, where he could jump three times as high as he could on Earth (but only half as high as he could on the Moon).

The Color of the Sky

Have you noticed the colors of the Martian sky? The paintings in this book try to show what the sky would really look like.

On Earth, our blue sky is created by the way sunlight passes through air. Most sunlight reaches the ground, but the air *scatters* a little bit of it in other directions. Without this light scattering, the sky would be pitch black, just like the sky on the Moon. Air scatters blue light more than light of other colors, which is why the sky is blue. (Remember that sunlight contains all the colors of the rainbow.)

On Mars, the air is so thin that, by itself, it would leave the sky nearly black even in the daytime. However, winds on Mars cause a lot of dust to be suspended in the Martian air. For much the same reason that dust and smog can make Earth's sky brownish, the suspended dust tends to give Mars the yellow-brown sky shown in most of the paintings. The sky color can differ in the mornings and evenings, and as the amount of suspended dust varies. All the colors shown in this book are at least somewhat realistic, with just a bit of artistic license.

After a while the astronauts began to take longer trips from base camp. They could travel for weeks in their pressurized rover. One of their first trips took them to an historical site — the robot rover named Spirit, which landed on Mars way back in 2004. It was still right where it had stopped many years ago, but it was now coated with Martian dust. Max regarded it warily, as if it might start rolling again at any moment.

Getting Around on Mars

Because Mars has as much land as all the continents on Earth combined, astronauts will need transportation to explore much beyond their landing site. In this story, the astronauts use a large, pressurized rover. It is as big as a bus, with beds, kitchen, and plenty of supplies so that the astronauts can live in it for weeks at a time. That way, they can take long journeys from their base camp.

Still, a rover probably won't allow trips longer than a few hundred miles, and some terrain will be too steep or rocky for a rover to cross. For example, the polar caps are probably among the most interesting plac-es on Mars, but Max and the crew don't visit them in this book because their rover can't go that far. (In fact, we've already taken art-istic license in having the crew visit places that are spread over a region a couple thou-sand miles across.)

The first human missions to Mars will pro-bably use rovers, just as in this story. Later missions might use airplanes, balloons, or rocket-powered vehicles to travel greater distances across Mars.

At every stop the crew collected rocks for scientific study. By figuring out what the rocks were made of and how long ago they formed, the astronauts learned about the history of Mars.

Max had a special job. His spacesuit had an attachment that let him sniff at rocks or the outside air. He was trained to bark if he caught the scent of any sign of life.

Commander Grant showed him rock after rock. Nothing . . . if there had ever been life here, Max wasn't finding it.

Could Max Really Search for Life?

This is a fictional story, and it's unlikely that a dog will really go on the first trip to Mars. Still, it's not a completely ridiculous idea. Just as Max does in this book, a dog could provide entertainment and comfort to astronauts on such a long trip away from home. It's even possible that a dog could be helpful in the search for life.

Dog noses are very sensitive. In many cases dogs have a better sense of smell than any machine we've yet been able to build. That's why police use dogs to sniff for missing people.

Of course, a dog couldn't go outside on Mars without a spacesuit, which is why Max's suit needs a special attachment to let him sniff. The attachment collects air and concentrates it, so that Max can sniff it without actually being exposed to the outside environment.

As the months passed, Max and the astronauts saw many amazing places on Mars. They spent weeks exploring the rim of the great Valles Marineris, a canyon that is almost as long as the United States is wide. The steep canyon walls dropped so far that it was difficult to see the bottom, and only in a few places could they see all the way across to the other side. In those places the view was stunning, especially in the morning when low clouds formed in the Martian sky.

A World of Wonders

Mars is a world of wonders. The painting on this page shows only a tiny part of Valles Marineris, which is actually several connected canyons that together make the largest canyon in the solar system. Unlike Earth's Grand Canyon, which was carved by a river, most of Valles Marineris was probably made by tectonic forces much like giant earthquakes. These forces may have cracked the Martian surface to create the canyons. Other Martian wonders include giant volcanoes, dried-up riverbeds, and ancient craters made long ago when asteroids or comets crashed down from space.

Mars also has a variety of climates and spectacular weather. Like Earth, Mars has polar ice caps, but they contain frozen carbon dioxide in addition to frozen water. Some of this carbon dioxide evaporates in spring and summer and then freezes again in winter, causing strong winds that sometimes generate huge, global dust storms. Clearly, Mars will be a favorite destination of thrill-seeking explorers of the future.

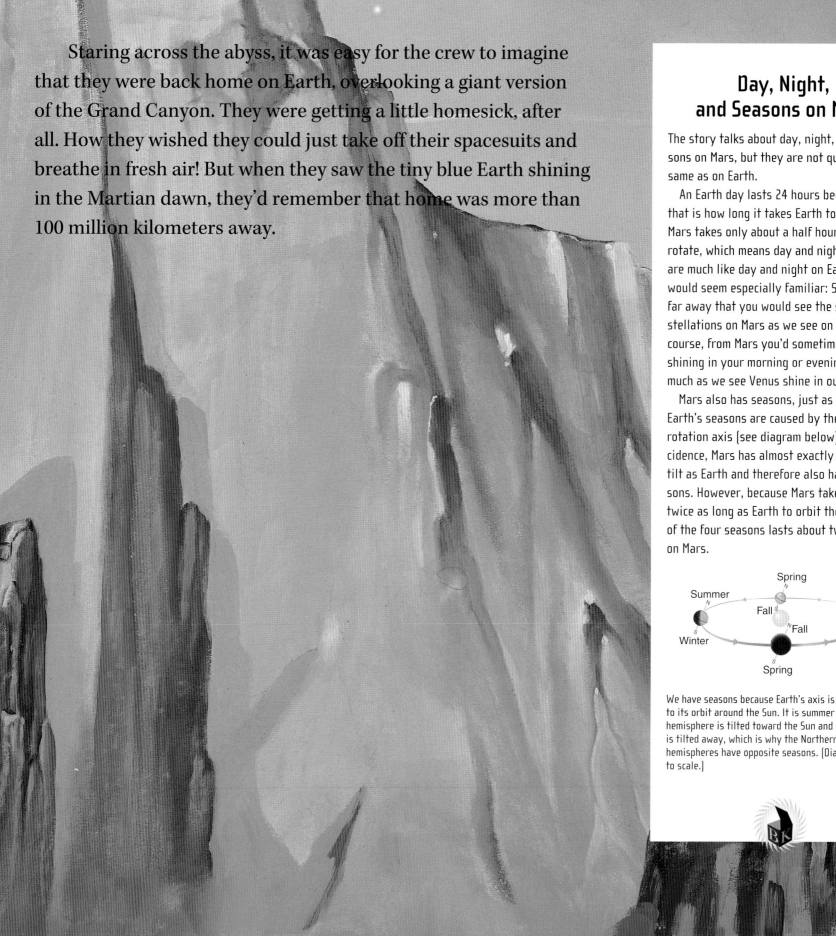

Staring across the abyss, it was easy for the crew to imagine that they were back home on Earth, overlooking a giant version of the Grand Canyon. They were getting a little homesick, after all. How they wished they could just take off their spacesuits and breathe in fresh air! But when they saw the tiny blue Earth shining in the Martian dawn, they'd remember that home was more than 100 million kilometers away.

Day, Night, and Seasons on Mars

The story talks about day, night, and seasons on Mars, but they are not quite the same as on Earth.

An Earth day lasts 24 hours because that is how long it takes Earth to rotate. Mars takes only about a half hour longer to rotate, which means day and night on Mars are much like day and night on Earth. Night would seem especially familiar: Stars are so far away that you would see the same constellations on Mars as we see on Earth. Of course, from Mars you'd sometimes see Earth shining in your morning or evening sky, much as we see Venus shine in our skies.

Mars also has seasons, just as Earth does. Earth's seasons are caused by the *tilt* of its rotation axis (see diagram below). By coincidence, Mars has almost exactly the same tilt as Earth and therefore also has four seasons. However, because Mars takes almost twice as long as Earth to orbit the Sun, each of the four seasons lasts about twice as long on Mars.

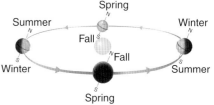

We have seasons because Earth's axis is tilted relative to its orbit around the Sun. It is summer when your hemisphere is tilted toward the Sun and winter when it is tilted away, which is why the Northern and Southern hemispheres have opposite seasons. (Diagram is not to scale.)

Olympus and Other Martian Volcanoes

Olympus Mons is indeed the biggest mountain in the solar system. It rises three times as high as Mount Everest stands above sea level on Earth, and its base covers an area as large as the state of Arizona. Despite its size, most of it slopes upward so gently that you could not see the summit from its base.

We know that Olympus Mons is a volcano because it has a huge caldera at its summit, and we can see where lava once flowed down its slopes. Mars also has many smaller volcanoes.

Martian volcanoes must have had spectacular eruptions in the past. Most of them are probably now extinct, meaning they no longer have enough heat for major eruptions. However, it's possible that some of the volcanoes may erupt again, though eruptions may come thousands or millions of years apart. More important to our story, some ancient volcanoes may still generate enough heat to melt underground ice and make pockets of liquid water beneath the Martian surface.

Olympus Mons, photographed from Martian orbit.

Their last planned outing took them to Olympus Mons, an ancient volcano that is the biggest mountain in the solar system. Max led the way as they hiked up the steep slopes around its base.

They had time to explore only a little bit of the great mountain before it was time for the long drive back to base camp. That was when disaster almost struck.

A huge Martian dust devil swept straight across the rover's path. Inside, it sounded like someone was sandblasting their car. They had to stop driving because they couldn't see anything out the windows. Luckily, the storm soon blew past. But they decided to alter their course to avoid other storms.

Their new route gave them the chance to make one last stop. It was an ancient river bed, not far from another volcano. They parked the rover and got out to explore.

And then it happened . . .

Martian Dust Storms

You may have seen dust devils on Earth. They look like little tornados, but they rise from the ground up rather than coming down from the sky. They happen when sunlight warms the ground enough to heat the air right above it, and the hot air begins to swirl as it rises upward. The swirling air can carry loose sand or soil, which is why dust devils are easiest to see over desert sands or dry farmland.

Dust devils are common on Mars, especially during summers, and they can be much bigger than dust devils on Earth. The swirling dust itself probably wouldn't be too dangerous, but it could cause problems by clogging engines or getting stuck in space-suit fittings. The dust devil in this story passes by without causing any problems for the rover, but real astronauts on Mars will need to be prepared to repair damage and clean off the dust left by dust devils.

Commander Grant nearly jumped out of his spacesuit when the sound of Max barking suddenly blasted into his earphones. He quickly turned and saw Max sniffing and digging at the dirt in the bottom of the dry river bed.

24

Commander Grant grabbed the drill and ran over to Max. He drilled down and down, bringing up rock from deep underground. It was wet!

Max and the crew returned to base camp as quickly as they could. In the base camp lab, Commander Grant used his microscope to look into the tiny, watery holes within the rock. He could barely contain his excitement as he realized what he was seeing. "Max," he shouted, "You did it! You discovered life on Mars!"

Is There Really Life on Mars?

Max finds life in this fictional story, but is there really life on Mars?

No one knows for sure, but most scientists doubt we'll find life on the surface of Mars, because of the lack of liquid water. All life on Earth needs liquid water to survive, so we suspect the same would be true of life on Mars. Also, because Mars lacks an ozone layer, ultraviolet radiation from the Sun would probably kill any unprotected life on the surface.

However, remember that Mars had abundant surface water in the distant past. Because water seems so important to life, it's possible that life got started on Mars at that time. If so, we might someday find fossils of ancient Martian life. Moreover, if Mars really did have life long ago, and if any liquid water remains underground, it's possible that some life still survives underground today, just as Max finds in this story.

To summarize, there are three possible answers to the question "Is there really life on Mars?" Mars may never have had life, it may have had life long ago that is now extinct, or it may still have life today. The only way we'll ever learn the correct answer is by continuing to explore the planet Mars.

25

Should We Send People to Mars?

In this book, people go to Mars not long after we return to the Moon, just as many people now hope. However, not everyone thinks it's a good idea to send people to Mars.

Sending people to Mars will be much more expensive than sending robotic spacecraft, so some people think we should stick with robots for that reason. Another concern is that people might actually hinder the search for life. You may not realize it, but your body is covered by trillions of microscopic bacteria. If you went to Mars, some of these bacteria would surely get outside and into the ground. Then if we found bacteria on Mars we might not know whether they were native to Mars or if they came from you. Also, like a weed that kills more valuable plants, there's at least a small chance that bacteria from Earth could endanger any native life on Mars.

Of course, the question of sending people to Mars is about more than science, because people have always had the urge to explore. It would surely be inspiring to see humans set foot on an entirely new world. So should we send people or not? You can decide what you think for yourself, but keep this in mind: If we decide to send people to Mars, the first trip will probably happen when kids now in school will be old enough to be astronauts. In other words, *you* could be the first person to set foot on Mars.

Max was a hero once again. On Earth, people planned celebrations to greet Max and the crew. On Mars, the crew prepared to leave. They made sure the base camp was properly closed, so it would be ready for the next Mars explorers. Then they returned to their rocket and blasted off for home.

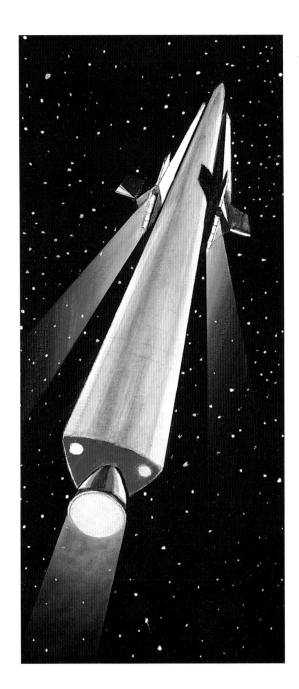

It took three months to reach the Moon, where doctors checked the crew for good health and scientists stored the Mars samples for future study. Then Max and the crew returned home to Earth.

Tori had missed Max so much! He'd been gone for more than two years, and she knew that he was getting old for a dog. She was very proud of him, and she wanted to treasure all the time he had left in his dog's life.

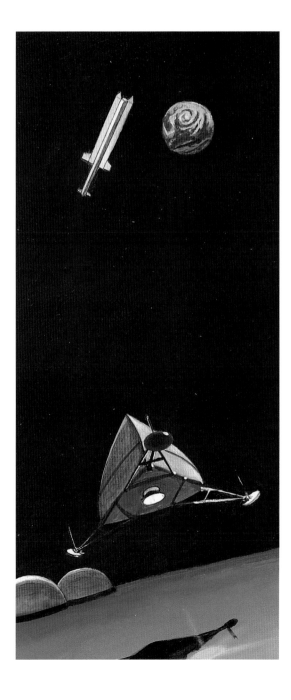

Dog Years, People Years, and Martian Years

By the time he's made trips to the Space Station, Moon and Mars, Max is getting old for a dog. But just how old is he? It depends on whether you want the answer in dog years, people years, or Martian years.

On Earth, a *year* really means only one thing: It's the time Earth takes to orbit the Sun, which is about 365¼ days. So if Max is 9 years old (the age of the real Max when this book was first written), it means Earth has circled the Sun nine times since he was born.

However, because dogs live much shorter lives than people, we sometimes talk about "dog years." There's no official definition for a dog year, but we usually say that one real year (or "people year") makes 7 dog years. So if Max is 9 real years old, he's $9 \times 7 = 63$ in dog years.

Of course, since Max goes to Mars in this story, we might also want to know his age in Martian years. Mars takes a little less than two Earth years to orbit the Sun, so his age in Martian years is about half his age in Earth years. If Max is 9 Earth years old, then he's 4½ Martian years old. How old are *you* in Martian years?

27

Max was glad to be back, too. He'd traveled farther and seen more than any dog in history. But he knew one thing as he looked out at the trees and squirrels and blue sky. There's no place like home and no planet like Earth.

Tori seemed to know what he was thinking. "Someday I'll make a trip to Mars too," she said, "and maybe even to planets beyond Mars. But I don't think we'll ever find another world quite as wonderful as this one."

29

Mars in the Night Sky

Diagram 1. The planetary motion demonstration. Follow the lines of sight from the inner person to the outer person to see where the outer person appears against the background. Notice that, as viewed from the inner person, the outer person appears to move backward between points 3 and 5.

Do you want to know why planets seem to wander through the constellations? Try this simple demonstration in which you pretend to be Earth and a friend pretends to be Mars.

Find a spot outside where you can put down a ball to represent the Sun. As shown in Diagram 1, you and your friend should both walk around the ball in the same direction (counterclockwise) so that you are like planets orbiting the real Sun. Your friend should walk more slowly and in a bigger circle than you, because Mars orbits the Sun more slowly and at a greater distance than Earth. Remember that each step represents a few weeks of real time, so you are demonstrating changes that occur over weeks and months, not over a single night.

Background trees or buildings can represent constellations, as long as you do one more thing: Pretend you don't realize that your friend (Mars) is closer to you than the constellations. Then your demonstration will be just like the night sky, in which we can't tell that planets are closer than stars just by looking.

Watch carefully as you walk several times around the Sun. Most of the time your friend will seem to move right to left through the background constellations. But during the times when you are "lapping" your friend, she'll seem to move backward (left to right) through the constellations, even though she's really still going in the

Answer to Challenge Question: Mars looks biggest and brightest when it is closest to us in its orbit, which is at Point 4 in Diagram 2. Notice that this is also right in the middle of its "backward" loop through the constellations.

same direction as you. Diagram 2 shows how the real Mars does the same thing as Earth laps it in its orbit.

Ancient people could not explain why Mars sometimes went backward through the constellations, because they thought the Sun, planets, and stars all went around the Earth. Today, as the demonstration shows, we know that the backward motion is just an illusion created by the way we view Mars as we orbit the Sun. This simple explanation for the backward motion played a very important role in human history: About 400 years ago, it was one of the major things that helped people realize that Earth is *not* the center of the universe and instead is a planet orbiting the Sun.

Challenge: At what point in Diagram 2 would Mars look biggest and brightest in our sky? (Answer at bottom of page 30.)

Diagram 2. The same idea explains the apparent motion of Mars. From Earth, we usually see Mars going from west to east through the constellations, but Mars seems to go backward as Earth laps it between points 3 and 5.

Mars Map

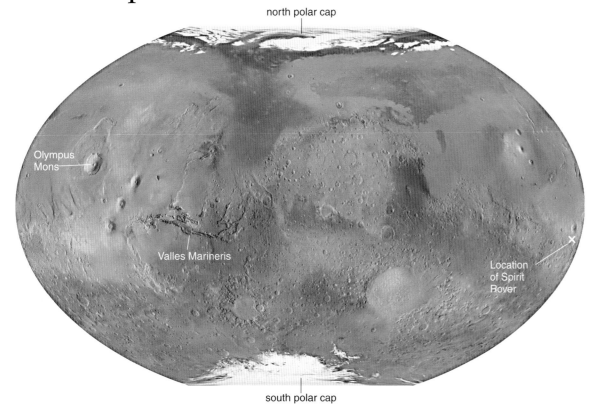

This map shows the full surface of Mars. You can see some of the places visited by Max and the astronauts in this story. Can you see some of the many impact craters on Mars? How many volcanoes can you spot in this picture?

A Note to Parents and Teachers
from the Author

Creating this new edition gives me the opportunity to address questions I've been asked during my many school presentations of the original edition and other books in the series. One of the most common questions, especially from parents and teachers, asks why I feel so strongly that we should send people back to the Moon, then onward to Mars and beyond.

The answer is simple: If we want kids to learn, we can't simply attempt to stuff information into their heads. Rather, we need to give them motivation to learn, using the triad I refer to as *education*, *perspective*, and *inspiration*. The education piece is the science (or other) content, the perspective piece involves seeing ourselves and our planet in a new light, and the inspiration piece comes in helping kids to dream of how much better the world could be if we all work together. In my opinion, there's no better way to put the three pieces together than through human space exploration. Robotic exploration can also provide education and new perspective, but no one grows up with the dream of being a robot. Inspiration comes from people.

The exploration of space is particularly inspiring, because it is a global endeavor to which scientists and engineers from virtually every nation, religion, and culture have contributed. There's nothing quite the same as being able to look up in the sky at a space station or a distant world and to think, "We all work together to go there, so surely we can work just as well together down here." That is why I believe human space exploration has the potential to inspire children not just to get an education, but also to work hard toward building a world in which we all live in peace and share in the advance of human knowledge.

Finally, I'll remind you that there are no real technological barriers to building a Moon colony today, and we could easily send people to Mars within the next couple of decades. The only thing missing is the will to make it happen. So the next time you look at your children, or other children you see at the park or playground or supermarket, don't forget this: *One of them could be the first person to walk on Mars.* Perhaps, as in this book, they might even be part of the team that answers once and for all the question of whether life exists beyond Earth. I hope this thought will inspire you to join in the effort to push space exploration forward, an effort that can literally set us on a path that will take our descendants to stars.

— Jeffrey Bennett

This photo, taken by the Curiosity rover on Mars, looks back at tracks left as the rover climbed a sand dune.